Self Witness to My Death and Burial

Victor Kabagi

Ukiyoto Publishing

All global publishing rights are held by

Ukiyoto Publishing

Published in 2023

Content Copyright © Victor Kabagi

ISBN

All rights reserved.
No part of this publication may be reproduced, transmitted, or stored in a retrieval system, in any form by any means, electronic, mechanical, photocopying, recording or otherwise, without the prior permission of the publisher.

The moral rights of the author have been asserted.

This is a work of fiction. Names, characters, businesses, places, events, locales, and incidents are either the products of the author's imagination or used in a fictitious manner. Any resemblance to actual persons, living or dead, or actual events is purely coincidental.

This book is sold subject to the condition that it shall not by way of trade or otherwise, be lent, resold, hired out or otherwise circulated, without the publisher's prior consent, in any form of binding or cover other than that in which it is published.

*I would like to dedicate this book to my younger cousins
Yvonne Vihenda and Innocent Buhilu.*

I would like to acknowledge the following, for their massive support, ranging from emotional, physically and financial: Margaret Kageha, Aunty Rose Kabagi and Briviern Jumba.

Contents

Self Witness To My Burial And Other Stories   1

The Enemy Of Independence   12

About the Author   *22*

Self Witness To My Burial And Other Stories

Twenty two years since my birth and now on the verge of going completely extinct. Hoping that the angel of doom won't delay nor hesitate to choose me. I've waited long enough for this terrifying journey so lustily and gluttonously. Some people said it was painful to die, others said it was a relief and that is why they usually wish the dead to 'rest in eternal peace'. They said it was heartbreaking to leave them behind and earnestly pleaded with me to hold on a little longer, at least for another one more week or month maybe but I was no longer in charge. Death was the captain now and the journey to a long desired eternity of peace had began.

I recall early that day in the hospital. Many people jostled in and out of this ward. Some came to bid their loved one's a quick recovery, some brought bouquet of flowers saying they were giving them some hope to cling on as they await the procedure, others brought food which on my side of view I didn't need to be told what it meant. I told myself it was the last supper for them because I was more than accurate that those patients were indeed taking their last meal in this vacuum world. There was no coming back for them. I witnessed some praying for their sick relatives and I nodded my head in unison probably because I understood without clarification that, it was the only password left in order to traverse to the other side of the universe.

However there was this irony with me. No one showed up even with an empty bowl. My ward mate too was alone. No one to console her except for the rhythmical music that was trying so hard to sooth her into eternal sleep, something that she said she was going to fight and eventually conquer. She never wanted to die, at least not this soon. She said she wanted to enjoy life. The difficult part was that, she was suffering from a throat cancer. She said through writing of course, that she had been used to smoking and drinking life that saw her lying almost lifeless in this hospital bed today.

She said her father was a drunkard, her mother a prostitute. She was lucky to be born in a family that glorified wine over food or beverage, which saw her landing her first and maybe her last job as bartender. She said she also multi tasked both in prostitution and a guardian of their already separated family. In her tone it was clear that she was not suffering from cancer alone, there were other dots of different illnesses including but not limited to HIV, that trailed her list. She looked goofy and emaciated. I'm not trying to justify myself because I was not better off either.

However, she was still determined to live, despite her health condition. She told me I was lucky to be dying peacefully. I stared blankly at her for a moment without saying a word. Had she known how my whole body looked like, she wouldn't have uttered what she uttered. How can you say am dying peacefully when my whole body is rotten? The only remaining healthy organ in me was my watery eyes and my pale face. She had hope. She said, if she happens to get out of this ward alive and kicking, the first thing she will do is to give her parents a good beating. Why? She said it will be one way of correcting them towards the path of proper parenting and child upbringing. Had her parents been responsible, she wouldn't be in here today and had they been more punctual and taken a short break from their drinking spree, she wouldn't have emulated their cracked footsteps and most probably not landed this dirty job. Her life would be better, and perhaps more advanced.

It was too late to regret now. I blame her for part of the consequences she's facing. One, because she was an adult when she first landed her nasty job. Secondly, experience is the best teacher, which means when she realized she had to multi task, she should have quit that job and concentrated on a more reasonable way of providing for her parents. Lastly, when she knew the cause of their parents' separation was alcohol, why didn't she quit drinking? Why couldn't she correct them? Why did she emulate them in the first place? I came to learn later on, that her name was Shaiffe'. "Do you fear that you might lose this war?" She asked me.

"No, am prepared. More so, everyone loses, eventually." I answered still unaware whether it was me talking or the morphine. My whole body was no longer in my charge. I was not feeling sick. Never had I laid on a hospital bed before, leave alone walking on the footpaths that led to the hospital. I always dreaded syringes and needles. The previous injections that I got when I was around five nearly killed me. I can't stand the double pain on my buttocks. I remember when someone who called himself doctor Saint came in the ward and told me that I was going to be getting four injections a day, I nearly shoved him through the window.

That is when he prescribed morphine for me. To reduce the excruciating pain. This happened for almost a week before I decided enough was enough. I grabbed the syringe from him and tried to get up forgetting my legs had already been amputated! I fell down carelessly, wondering what was happening to me. Shaiffe' watched in horror the unprecedented movie with eyes of disbelief. Nurses later came and helped me back to bed. I never saw doctor Saint again and concluded maybe he was a Saint from hell.

"Don't you hope for the best? There's a brighter tomorrow you know?" She tried teasing me as big lumps of tears frequented her dim eyes. It was as if I was the decoy of my body and she was my real body that felt all the sickness.

"Of course I do, but those days are over. For now I just hope you'll be there to witness my burial and give me a better sendoff. I'm proud of you Shaiffe'. I know there's happiness where am heading because this journey requires that you have internal toughness but the outer layer belongs to the sacred soil that we were modelled from. Remember we were created from the same dust but different souls".

"Do not say such horrible things please...look, here I am suffering from throat cancer, but I have immeasurable faith and hope that all this shall come to pass soon, and I shall reunite with 'them' again. Just hold on a little longer okay?" She pleaded with me tearfully and sorrowfully as if her existence depended solely on mine. We were just two strangers, different backgrounds. She was white, I was black. The only common thing here was the same African hospital and the same ward which made us ward mates in a prison called hospital.

I saw no need to argue about false hope. I knew all this time, I was not the one doing the talking; morphine was representing my mouth temporarily, before eternal sleep could overtake it completely. She was my only friend in this time of departure. To her, I was a companion upon life's way. "I'm sorry for you. I didn't know you were going through such horrendous pain. I wish you well and hope that you come out of this hospital victorious, which I'm sure with your undying determination and brevity of heart and soul, you'll make it happen". I said faintly.

"Okay, but you have to be strong. Will you be saying such things to your parents when they come visiting?" She asked amidst sobs.

"Luckily, they won't hear me saying because none is coming ". I assured her.

"Why? Why won't they be coming?" She asked very shocked.

"Because they do not exist?" I told her plainly.

"Am sorry then, but if you don't mind, just tell me are your parents dead? How about your sisters, brothers...uh?" She nagged me.

I thought for a moment about revealing to her about everything but my conscience could not allow me. I even thought of lying to her but I saw no need to do so, since I had only a few moments before I could go into a permanent sleep. I had to at least use those few minutes to tell the truth. It was the last law of death, that a dying man, lies not. I summoned my last remaining strength that could barely allow me to say more than twenty words.

"It is twenty two years since I saw them. That is all..." I said this and went mute, allowing the last drop of tear to speedily race down my dry cheekbones. "Hey, tell me what happened" pleaded Shaiffe' worriedly, but that nothing came out of my mouth again, not even a sigh. " When she felt my pulse, she realized that my body was cold. "No! Don't tell me you're no more! Doctor! Doctor! She yelled out loudly as she drew closer to my bed, shaking it vigorously. The next day, I found myself in the morgue. The serenity and calmness in here, was frightening. I understood that this was the second step before reaching the slumber land.

My body was washed by a fierce looking man. He didn't care if he was hurting me or not. He was doing his job. This brought a question I never expected to jot in my mind that moment. Does he think he is a god? That he will never die someday? Even immortals do die eventually, who does he take himself for? Scrubbing and punching the dead, just because they're dead? I witnessed how he slapped me in the face just because the tray I was lying on could not move in conjunction with that of his big hands and palms.

I knew, I will get back to him someday, when he will come 'visiting' and I will avenge myself for having humiliated me on my way to rest. When he was done, he shoved me into a cold box and straight away into the fridge! I stayed in there for three days without seeing anyone. The only thing that I heard was footsteps of morgue attendants with their client's who had come to pick their dead loved ones. Mine was picked the fourth day in the wee hours of dawn. Their intention most probably was to lay me to rest early enough before the sunset.

I was clothed in a three-piece black suit and a pearl white shirt. I resembled an angel! I was happy and mad at the same time. How could they buy me a new suit when am dead? What was the goodness in putting new wine into an old wineskin? They disappointed me, but then I was happy that for the first time in my life or death, I had worn a suit. I was going under, in a suit. I was then put in a comfortable coffin and off, we drove home in a pick up.

Back home, my ancestral home that is, masses of people had gathered in small groups, discussing about my sudden demise in low tones. When we entered the compound, cries and screams filled the air. There are those who cried bitterly than others. I couldn't tell why, maybe I had taken with me something they valued, into the slumber land. I wondered what I had done wrong. I could hear whisper's and murmurs about how hardworking I was, from those who knew me well from my childhood days. I saw my aunt whom I had been referring to, as my mother when I was alive some few days ago.

She wept bitterly, maybe because we had spent so many years together and all that time she had taken me as her own son. Having passed on at a tender age, meant a great loss to her and her life in particular. I had been a great companion of hers in those useful days. I recall a text I read from my long reserved diary books which said; "someday, some thankless mouths will surely say, his useful days are surely over". Before I could finish alluding this text, I heard someone whom I had known for a long time saying the exact words from the diary. He was my former classmate, from my high school days. It appeared to me that I was receiving my dues for what I had done to them when I was still with them, but then I realized there's a time I heard someone saying every living thing, be it animal, man or plant, will have to taste death at least once in their lifetime. This was my turn, theirs was in the looming. What I was not sure of was, when?

This revitalized me a little, to continue witnessing my own burial ceremony, from where I lay still in my carefully and skillfully carved, wooden coffin with a glass cover on top. I saw my elder sister. The way she moved her fingers to touch my forehead, forgetting the glass shield that acted as a barrier between my body and her. A steaming hot teardrop fell on the glass causing a mass of moisture, which she quickly wiped and walked away stealthily. Why did we have to meet in death? Why didn't she ever come to visit me both when I was alive and in the hospital? Where was she all these twenty two years? I wondered. She must have been shocked about my demise at this young age, but the question still remains where were they when I needed them the most? I was not trying to revenge by dying. It was my turn now and theirs was to come...

Many came to view my lifeless carcass, giving their last respects to it. Some also brought large bouquet of wreaths and flowers especially roses and lavender. It became evident to me that people only value you and see you as of great worth when you're gone. When you have left a gap that none of them is worthy of filling. It is true that we become old too early and wise too late, to never appreciate a person's worth when they still dwell among us.

They sung melancholic and somber filled songs that only meant one thing; to appease and sooth my dead body and spirit, since they believed that when a person dies, only the body dies but the spirit and the soul move to another realm. At least they were right on this one because I could attest to it. Food and other delicacies were served in humble measure and with gratitude.

They ate and got satisfied. I also enjoyed because while they ate the actual food, I was busy consuming the aroma. It seems I was somehow rejoicing in my death, because at least for once again in my life and death, I was able to unify such a great multitude of people from both gender, race and class. I was also able to eat the rare meal that I have always longed for.

There came this time, when cries intensified. They became louder than before. I didn't know what was happening but I began to feel weak and lonely again. That is when I understood the meaning of the statement I had given Shaiffe' back in the ward... "No, am ready, everyone loses eventually..." Cries became immense, which gave me a thought that maybe somebody else had died but that was not the case. I saw someone closing the coffin lid and the coffin started moving! They were taking me to my resting place; the grave! I recall this wonderful song in Swahili, which they sung repeatedly and somberly. It went;

> Eh, bwana u' niinue
>
> Kwa Imani, nisimame
>
> Niipande mi'lima yote
>
> Eh, bwana u' nipa'ndishe

A hot tear dropped from the corner of my already shut eye, rolling all the way down into my left ear. After matching for a while, we arrived at the graveyard and the coffin was placed on the casket lowering system. There followed a moment of silence then a short prayer from Father Simon.

"Dear Father, we pray that his soul may rest in eternal solace; ashes to ashes, soil to soil and dust to dust, Amen". The crowd put a big amen to seal the prayer, as he sprinkled few handfuls of red mound onto the coffin. This time I was enclosed in a dark coffin. It was clear to me that this was the final goodbye to them. The more the spades of soil landed into the grave the fainter my hearing ability became, until I could hear nothing anymore. I just gasped out of energy but not before I could say," Thanks for a nice burial".

The Enemy Of Independence

There existed this enemy that everyone was humming about. This is the enemy that chocked people, murdered them at will, crucified others, strangled others and made all of them slaves of man. It was double edged blade kind of thing, that cut both sides; the guilty and the righteous, the poor and the rich but mostly, overwhelmed those who could not control their existence in this cruel and beast dominated world.

The beast that ran deep in the wealthy merchant's souls. It fed them of greed, hate, resentment, ego and above all, made them enslavers of their very own people. You cannot stop a hungry beast for a better life. To be honest, this very enemy of the people was neither transparent, translucent nor opaque. It was invisible yet existent. It had no stomach and was mouth less, yet it drank and fed on people's flesh and blood without for once getting satisfied or quenching it's thirst. On the contrary, it kept on desiring for more and more blood while its appetite grew at an astounding rate.

However this enemy was not one or two but three. Yes, there were three of them, that had vandalized, terrorized, rendered captive, murdered, torched and erased from existence, the hope, the value and the human dignity that once reigned in the hearts of the people of Kenya.

There happened to be a leader who appeared to the people once during the struggle. He came to unify, something he referred to as 'Liberation'. He had come to join and lead them into a fight for a promising, eye opener and perhaps the light of the nation and the country to be. He was both an animal and human. Spiritually, he was hungry for freedom. Mentally, he was blazing and fuming for liberation of his country people. Physically, he was prepared to see the white man out of the Kenyan house. His name became Kenyatta, and the country became Kenya.

What did he come to do? Why did he act like a person suffering from a multi personal disorder? Who was he as a human being and who was he as an animal? Many questions erupted and flooded the minute minds of the doubtful 'people of the nation', as he referred to them. Who was he as an animal? He lived and dwelt in the caves and trees. With a huge beard and moustache, long hair, a dark skin as the continent itself, it was with this unique features that landed him the beautiful name, 'African'. He was an animal as the whites referred to him. This is because of the skin cloaks that he majorly put on.

This landed him the famous name that he proudly started identifying himself with and the one that brought about the brilliant name of this very country , that he came to redeem, deliver from harsh rule and liberate the inhabitants, together as one. 'Kenyatta' his name went and 'Kenya' his country became. Africa was his central abode and he was the proudest son of this beloved motherland called Africa. He was a strong animal-human during the whites reign. His die hard spirit was a stumbling block to the white men who began to stumble even on pebbles.

As a human to his fellow black men, he was a well nurtured African child. Born and brought up by the Kenyan people. He was a leader and a hope to the yet to be declared an independent country. He was the liberating father of all Kenyan communities. His mixed personality worked to the advantage of his fellow country people. When he intermingled with the 'real people', as the whites referred to themselves, he was a cunning fox. He stole their every tactic, which he later on, would come to use against them, but when he walked among his people, he became the lion that groaned in pain and anguish of extreme harsh treatment from the superior whites. The wounds that he understood, were not going to probe, not in the near future.

The itching of those wounds were a constant reminder to him that, he had to pursue this course ahead of him, with diligence and brevity of heart for the betterment of a relieving, promising and a fruitful tomorrow. He was the only antidote to the ferocious, fierce, greedy and ready to devour upon getting the slightest chance type of enemy called cowardice and superiority complex.

This was his field of renovation. To fight the enemy of cowardice out of African- Kenyans. He was the enlightenment to the Kenyan people in this stone age era, when the natives still dwelt in caves and holes of fear, submission oppression and constant humiliation in the hands of the so-called superior whites.

He was the Mandela of Kenya and not Iddi Amin of Uganda. He was seeking to restore the African dignity and create a conducive society for all to dwell without hiccups of fear or war. He brought enlightenment through basic books, to curb away cowardice of superiority complex and insufficient knowledge among Kenyans. He also fought it through teaching them how to write and read. He said there was time to read and time to write and also time to draw and time to sketch the African heritage. By this, he meant to watch out for the White's tactics and time to attack and also retreat. He also taught the survival. He taught them in every way possible, both action and practical, theory and in statement.

He proved to them that also this very beings who called themselves superior, felt pain just like they did. He told them, they were no lesser beings than they. They bled, they felt pain and they cried just like them. All these, he did to scrape of fear among them. This he finally achieved through the first liberation of Mau Mau fighters.

The full enlightenment came after the hard battle, that was almost calling upon Africans to surrender, but he led them through. Fighting hard the spirit of timidity and self doubt among Kenyans. He became weak at some point but he was motivated by other African liberators like Oginga Odinga, James Gichuru, Kimathi Dedan, among others. He was on the verge of losing, until when the white flag which had dominated them for decades, finally gave up and got torn into pieces, out of exhaustion from having oppressed Kenyans for so long. That is when the whites knew, they were no longer needed in the country. Now the smell of liberation lingered in the acrid smoke. Independence was now at hand and ready to serve with justice. Spears and gunfire collided in the smoky air causing lumps of fire everywhere. It was a smoking country. Chaos of immediate departure could be seen and heard. " Independence at last" he sighed with relief at his achievement. He had fought a good fight and finished the race, but where was he all these past years of suffering? But he still remained the father of this proud Nation.

There emerged another enemy. Monster like but also ghost like. It manifested in many forms; money, power, lust and thirst. To begin with, lust drifted in air like a hot air balloon that was taking geographical measurements. Lust was tempting, deceitful and destructful. It was then fueled by hate, pride, resentment and later bore disagreements. It the found a home. A very tidy home in the hearts and souls of Kenyan people; poor, fragile to its gimmicks and innocent minds. God created man, man made technology and later that same innovation came back to destroy him.

Man, in this case an African, who did not understand anything about metal currencies was an easy to find bait. Lust had engulfed him into a dark hole of corruption. This is the very enemy that the second legend came to eradicate but he came too late. It had deepened its roots in people's souls. Man killed man. It was a man eat man literally, kind of society. He had diverted his mind and soul from hunting the wild animals; an enemy of his, in the wilderness called home, and changed his role to man eater.

What did it benefit him? Why did he do it? When did he start killing fellow people? All these questions reflected towards only one thing: an enemy of development. A debacle of progress. When did he start killing fellow people? Good question. It all began when and during the first liberation. When the African cowardice had been torched by the first liberator. Now with the white man gone, Kenyans organized themselves on how to take the country forward, in the very style and way, that they had always wanted and wished. They found treasures hidden in large wooden boxes, in the 'used to be' bungalows of their predecessors. They had gold, diamonds, dynamites, copper coins and granite among other treasures. They also came across the armory that consisted of long guns and gun powders. So man became unbeatable, unshakeable and indestructible mainly because he had everything under his command.

Man killed his fellow for want of more wealth. Greed had gotten better of him. Where there is lust, there exists hate, pride and ego. The spices that stirred up the burning and ardent aroma to terminate in order to avoid sharing of the very small fortune. What did it benefit him? Now with a full ecosystem, the prey and predator arrived earnestly in the field of survival. It was eat or be eaten kind of existence. This meant, whatever small one had, they had to fight to keep it, or give it up to the rightful owner.

The last question comes…why did he do it? Now with the monster having found a home in him, it had built cobwebs of strife, chaos and more lust. He was its servant and it, his master. His mind and soul, was now oozing of moral rottenness, and the society was on the edge. This was the second time independence was going to hurt them. Some said, Africans had championed for the African flag and not the independence itself. It was the same with Kenyans. The actual control and administration was still with the whites and Kenyans, their footstool. He had become a slave once again, to his very enemy.

He had found power, that is a share in governance but under the true leadership of the very colonialist they had smoked out of the country. With a portion of power,he felt very proud and gained fame. The very ingredients that led him to become a white man's puppet, because they knew he was still the same 'ape', only the forest had shifted. There came an antidote to this malady but it was never effective. Bribing for public services became rampant, crimes were on the surge. High officials in government committed all sorts of crimes ranging from rape, murder, fornication, embezzlement of public funds, misuse of public offices. Surprisingly, all these crimes went unpunished as water slips through the fingers in unforgiving desert. The innocent remaned to be sacrificial lambs while wolves were let loose to roam in power and governance. The poisoned Kenyan leader fed his fellows of the same concoction even when he knew that they were going to die, but that is what they wanted, what they had championed for.

A clean nation without poverty and uncountable mouths to feed; a nation with no competition for the available scarce resources. It was liberty for those already liberated but for the lowly Kenyans, and Africans in general, they still were in the darkest caves of evolution, what the liberated called, 'stone age era'.

There descended into power, the man slayers. Do not ask how they got there; of course through corruption and bribery but fortunately they were our own Kenyans baptized to be in government to fight for our interests. The likes of Tom Mboya, Kung'u Karumba, Achieng Oneko and Oginga Odinga. Loyal they were to the diligent course. Their aim to 'clean' the government in whichever way they could. They first demanded more seats in parliament, then came the fair pay and later demanded to run the government businesses on their own. The aim being to completely eradicate the colonialist from power.

They said even if it was going to cost them their lives, they would rather stumble on pebbles and rise up again till they reached the peak, than handing full Kenyan control into foreign hands. They termed it as allowing hyena to herd sheep in the grazing field with a sinister mentality that the hyena will not pounce on a sheep just because he pretented to be vegetarian. The colonialists wanted the country to be a one party state, for easy administration but that was contrary to the Kenyan leaders. They wanted more channels from which to quench their thirst. They therefore went for diplomacy and force, divide and rule type of strategy, forcing kenyans to pay taxes, among other things. How different were they from the colonial administration? Why enslave a fellow African in their own country?

Now with those days long gone. Laws to curb corruption having been implemented, the country is now hanging on the knot, that had long been tied, most probably because they knew danger was in the looming, seizing an opportune time to strike and that explains the reason for the long tied knot. There came this last leader. He said he was championing for the second liberation. What relevance was this constitution to us? They would ask. Why does it show up now? It was evident that things happen for a reason and at the right time.

What and who is it for? Kenyans of course! He said this liberation was to make Kenyans aware of their rights and freedoms. He stated that even the deadly criminals had rights and freedoms. He said they deserved to coexist peacefully, harmoniously as they serve their sentences. This liberation, he said was to envelop all forms of corruption murder and other criminal offenses.

Why does it come up now? Angry Kenyans asked. The age of stone age era was over! He said. Now with the enlightenment from the first liberation that was championing for independence gone and the second one on the door, he said, was going to bring drastic changes in the lives of kenyans. Cowardice having been erased, even though not completely, the country had began a long journey to its dreams fulfilment.

What was its relevance? They cried. He said it was a long term solution to a long time maniac that had oppressed and vandalized them for decades. The giant that had forced some to be the sacrificial lambs for other people's wrongdoings. No one was going to go unpunished for their crimes. It was a fair judge that saw the rich and the poor face the rightful arm of the law. Despite the rich and high officials having implemented the laws, they ended up being the victims of the very law they drafted. A country that is unable to protect its citizens, is not a country but a zombie world, where the same country feeds on its young ones.

The power of the new dawn, new power, new constitution and new people. A day of delight in the hands of the faithful bondservants, citizens and all the inhabitants. The new constitution had done it all!

About the Author

Victor Kabagi

Kabagi Victor is a young Kenyan author, whose work lies solely in poetry, fiction romance, thriller and mystery. His works of fiction include: Tentacles of Love, Unquenchable Tears, The Killer Coin, African Whispers, The Smoke, and When the Light Fades. He currently works as an automotive engineer with a private company.

www.ingramcontent.com/pod-product-compliance
Lightning Source LLC
LaVergne TN
LVHW041602070526
838199LV00046B/2095